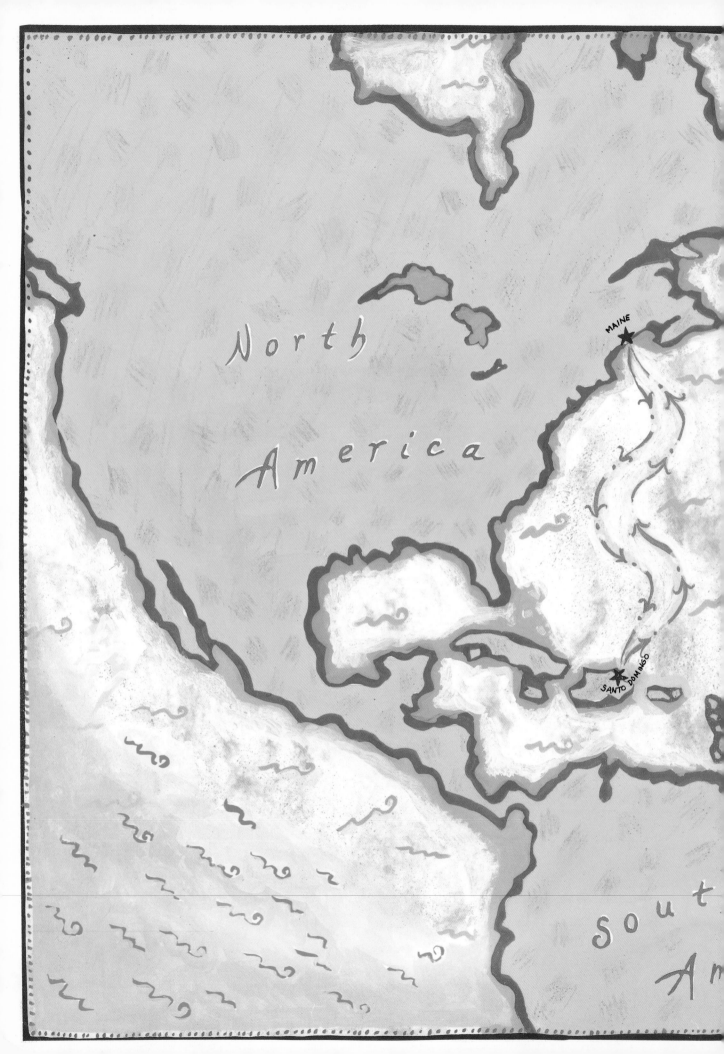

For Avigail, who asked me to write for children —D.A.

*The pictures in this book I dedicate to
J. Joanne Meade, my mother, whose
support and quiet strength continue
to hold me up. —H.M.*

Text copyright © 1997 by Diana Appelbaum

Illustrations copyright © 1997 by Holly Meade

Orchard Books
95 Madison Avenue
New York, NY 10016

Manufactured in Singapore
Printed by Toppan Printing Company, Inc.
Book design by Chris Hammill Paul

10 9 8 7 6 5 4 3 2 1

The text of this book is set in 15 point Goudy Sans and 15 point Goudy.
The illustrations are cut paper and gouache.

Library of Congress Cataloging-in-Publication Data

Appelbaum, Diana Karter.
    Cocoa ice / by Diana Appelbaum ; pictures by Holly Meade.
        p.   cm.
    Summary: A girl in Santo Domingo tells how cocoa is harvested during the
late 1800s while at the same time her counterpart in Maine tells about the harvesting
of ice.
    ISBN 0-531-30040-4. — ISBN 0-531-33040-0 (lib. bdg.)
    [1. Chocolate—Fiction. 2. Ice—Fiction.] I. Meade, Holly, ill. II. Title.
PZ7.A6415Co 1997
[E]—dc21   96-40365

COCOA ICE

By **DIANA APPELBAUM**
Pictures by **HOLLY MEADE**

Orchard Books

New York

Chocolate comes from a faraway island where birds have pink feathers, leaves grow bigger than I am tall, and it is always summer. Children who live on the island never have to wear boots or clean ashes from the stove because winter never comes. Best of all on the island of always-summer, chocolate grows on trees.

The island where chocolate grows on trees is called Santo Domingo and I know all about it because Uncle Jacob sails there on a trading schooner. Once, he brought home a seashell for the mantel shelf. Inside it is pink and smoother than anything in the world. If you hold it to your ear, it whispers, "Summer . . . summer . . . summer. . . ."

COCOA

Early morning is the best time to climb a tree because the sun has not yet had time to bake the earth until it is hot and steamy like a roasted plantain. If you wait until afternoon, rain will make the trees too slippery to climb. But if you get up while the birds are looking for their breakfast and sit absolutely still, one may come so close that you can feel its feathers ruffle the air. Still, the main reason why morning is the best time to climb to the top of a very tall tree is that if a schooner comes into the bay, you will be the first to see it.

We have every kind of tree around our house: coconut, papaya, mango, orange, banana, plantain, breadfruit, guava, and a special kind called cacao — trees that grow chocolate. Cacao trees grow only in shade, so Papa plants young cacaos under tall banana trees that shade the growing cacao.

Little pink cacao flowers grow right on the trunk. Green cacao pods grow side by side with the flowers, and next to them grow ripe yellow and red pods, ready to be picked. A cacao tree is always blooming, always ripening, and always ready to harvest.

Papa splits the ripe cacao pods
open with his machete and scoops
out white pulp and pale beans. We
spread slippery beans and sticky-
sweet pulp on a carpet of banana
leaves, then cover everything with
more banana leaves.

I like to eat the sweet cacao pulp
while we work, but I don't chew the
beans! Once I bit a fresh cocoa
bean. It was so bitter it set my teeth
on edge. Papa laughed and said,
"Don't be so impatient, little one.
Wait for the sun to make
chocolate." And it does.

After a few hot days under the
banana leaves, the pale, bitter cocoa
beans begin to change color. We
pick beans out of the old, smelly
pulp and spread them to dry in the
sun, turning them until they
become a dark, beautiful brown.

Today the cocoa beans are drying. There is no work to do in the garden, and Papa says we are going conching. Mama wraps cassava bread in banana leaves and packs it in a basket with guavas for our lunch. It's hot paddling down the river San Juan, and we have a long way to go because after the river reaches the sea we must paddle along the beach until we reach a cove sheltered from ocean waves. I'm tired and thirsty when we finally pull the canoe onto the beach, so Papa opens coconuts and we drink their sweet milk. Now it is time to hunt for conchs.

I push my basket into the water and wade out until slippery leaves of turtle grass brush against my legs. Conchs are hiding in the turtle grass. Swimming slowly, I push the grass aside. Conchs look a lot like mossy rocks when they stand still, but I'll catch one if it hops.

Something moves under the grass and I dive for it, surfacing with the conch and looking for Papa to show him my catch. But as I reach to put my prize in the basket, a big, red claw reaches for me! I squeal and drop the fierce shell. It's only a hermit crab. But I want conchs, not hermit crabs.

Mama lets me have the shells after she steams the conchs and picks the meat out for chowder. I line them up in the sunny clearing where we dry cocoa beans. After they have sat in the sun for a few days, I can brush off the sea moss that made the shells look like dull green rocks in the turtle grass, and see them glisten in the sunshine. Inside they are pink like cacao flowers, but smooth and shiny even after they're dry.

Our beans are not chocolate yet;
they are only cocoa beans and we
must turn them every day until they
are dry. Mama roasts them over a
hot fire until they begin to smell like
chocolate. Then she lets me put
them in the mortar and crush them.
The best thing about being allowed
to pound cocoa beans is the
chocolate smell that curls up to
your nose.

We put the crushed cocoa beans into a chocolate pot. While Mama boils the water, pours it over the beans, and adds sugar, I set out the cups. I think hot chocolate is the most wonderful drink in the whole world. Unless there is an ice schooner in the bay.

When a schooner comes, Papa drags his canoe to the river. It took a long time to hollow the canoe out of a log and Papa is very careful never to drag it over a rock.

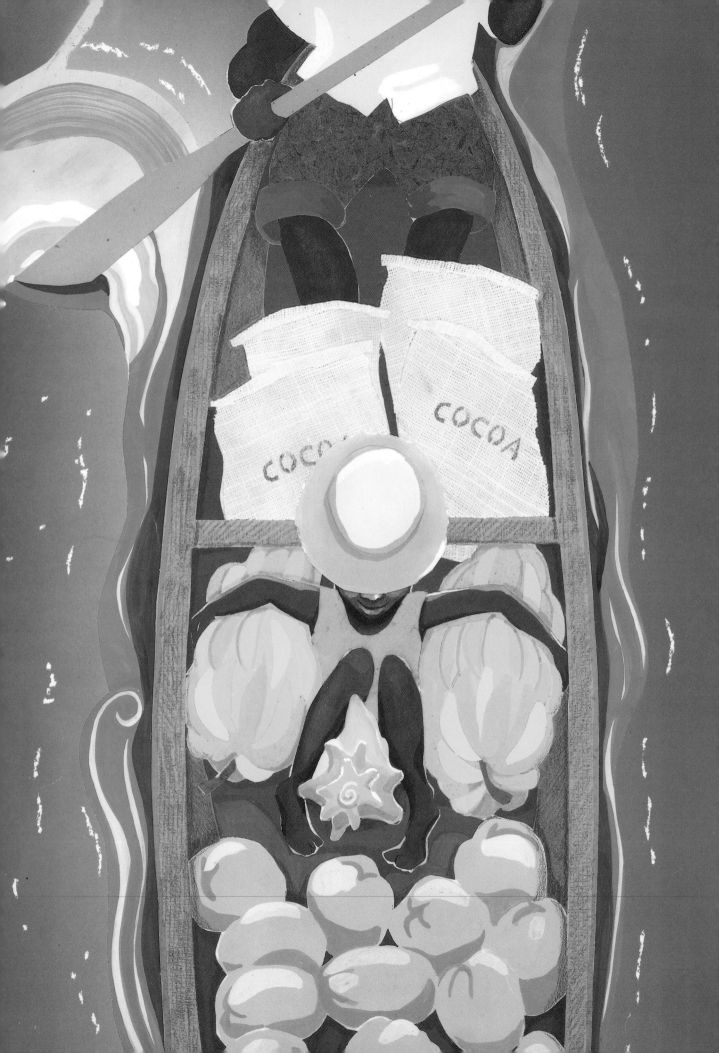

We pile the sacks of dried cocoa beans into the canoe, along with a heap of coconuts and bananas. I climb in between two bunches of bananas as big as I am, settle my best conch shell between my feet, and we're on our way.

Papa carries me up the side of the ship on a rope, and one of the sailors leans down to lift me over the rail. Other families have come and Papa must wait his turn to trade with the captain. Clutching my conch shell, I search the crowd for the sailor named Jacob who once showed me pictures of his faraway country. He spots me first, and says hello with a big smile.

I show Jacob my beautiful conch shell and let him feel how smooth and pink it is inside. He shows me a picture of a girl, just my age, with a ribbon in her hair. Then he pulls a small, square bag with stitching on it from his pocket. Jacob holds the bag to his face, sniffs it, and smiles. I sniff too. It doesn't smell like chocolate or jasmine or papaya or anything in the world. It smells strange and wonderful. And now it's mine.

Papa trades too. I know he must bargain for a bolt of cloth, but I hop with pleasure when I see what else Papa has traded our cocoa beans for. ICE!

The sailors lower a block of ice into our canoe and Papa covers it with banana leaves. Then they hand me over the rail and, when I am settled, one of them passes down the new cloth. I put it carefully into a dry basket. Holding the bag with the wonderful smell safely in my lap, I wave good-bye to Jacob, the *marinero*.

When we get home, Mama scoops sweet, white pulp from a ripe cacao pod and beats it smooth and soft. Then she shaves the ice, stirs it into the cacao pulp, and pours it into cups for us to drink.

Cocoa ice is white and sweet and so cold I think it must be magic. It slides down my throat and makes me shiver to think of children living in such an icy place.

Ice schooners come from a land where the water is so hard that people walk on the river — right on the river. This place where water turns into ice is called Maine, and I know all about it because the sailor Jacob showed me pictures. In Maine the people build cooking fires inside their houses and the trees don't have any leaves. And now I know another thing about Maine. I know that it has a wonderful smell. I sniff my balsam bag and try to imagine a land where children walk on rivers of ice.

ICE

Winter grips Maine hard. The days are short, bright, and so cold that sometimes nothing moves, not the wind, not the birds, not even the river.

But our kitchen is warm. Mama bakes apple pies in the big stove and I practice my stitching by making a balsam pillow with fir needles. Papa and Uncle Jacob work for the ice company. If they can fill the big icehouses before spring breakup, Uncle Jacob's schooner and other ships can carry pieces of Maine winter to sell in hot countries far away. That's why we worry about snow.

Papa and Uncle Jacob and I stand on the riverbank stamping our boots, watching snow fall on new ice, and worrying.

"Figure it'll hold?" Papa asks, looking over the thin sheet of ice.

Uncle Jacob doesn't answer. They both know that air in the pockets of a million snowflakes will keep the river from freezing, and unless the river freezes there will be no ice to sell. But this ice is new and too thin to scrape. It has to be tapped — if it will hold the weight of a man.

We watch Uncle Jacob slide a wide plank onto the snowy surface and step out onto the river. It holds.

Soon a line of men follows Uncle Jacob. They inch forward, tapping holes in the ice with needle bars and mallets. River water seeps up through the holes, turning powder snow into a soggy slurry. If the weather stays cold, the icy water will freeze solid — thick enough to support a horse.

Horses are important once the ice is thick enough to scrape. After every snowstorm Papa and Uncle Jacob harness our teams to heavy snow scrapers and clean snow off the river so the ice can freeze thick and clear. From Augusta all the way to Merrymeeting Bay, men and teams scrape snow to help the river freeze.

One morning when the sky is clear and there is no snow to scrape, Papa takes the wheels off the wagon box and puts the runners on. Mama bundles us in extra hats and mittens, and tucks us into a pile of hay under a heavy quilt. Riding in a wagon on runners is like flying; we fly upriver clear to the falls! It's so cold that by morning the river has frozen more than a foot thick. Time to fill the icehouses.

I watch the ice boss rule a straight line across the river as though he were getting ready for a giant arithmetic lesson. Papa follows that line with the big ice cutter. The cutter's steel teeth slice through solid ice as easy as a knife slicing through Mama's apple pie, but Papa is careful not to cut through to the water. The ice has to stay solid enough to walk on until the whole surface has been grooved and cut into blocks. Back and forth they go, grooving and cutting until the river looks like a giant checkerboard, only — all the squares are white.

Fifty men are at work on the river today, grooving, cutting, sawing, and barring off blocks of ice, floating them across open water, pushing them into place on the elevator chain that lifts them toward the open door of the great icehouse. The upper doors are higher than the roof of the church, and the ice boss aims to fill it to the rafters before breakup.

I watch until I get so cold I have to run into the kitchen. Mama makes hot chocolate to warm me up.

Ice isn't worth anything unless you can get it all the way to summer without melting. That's why icehouse walls are built double, two walls with a wide space between, filled with sawdust to keep the cold in. That's why even icehouse doors are built double and filled with sawdust to keep summer out. And why we insulate the ice with a blanket of sweet meadow hay. When Uncle Jacob cuts the bales open, the green smell of summer meadows spills from the hay and fills the loft.

The men fill the great building one room at a time, lining blocks of ice up in perfect rows. Straight lines of ice that reach from wall to wall and rise in towers until they almost touch the roof. After the icehouse is full, the boss closes the doors and waits for the river to break up.

No matter how cold winter is, summer always comes. New grass in the pasture feels soft on my toes, and schooners come back up the Kennebec. Sailors fill the holds with ice, pouring a thick layer of sawdust all around as they stack it, and covering the sawdust with hay from our meadows.

Mama says ice from our river goes halfway around the world in ships that come home filled with silk and cashmere, ginger and tea. But the most important ship of all is the ice schooner Uncle Jacob is sailing on today, bound for Santo Domingo to bring home chocolate.

I give Uncle Jacob the sweet-smelling balsam pillow I made to carry with him to the island of always-summer, and wave until his schooner disappears around the bend. I can't stop crying.

Mama says, "I think this would be a good day to make ice cream."

Opening the icehouse door in summer is like stepping into the castle where winter fell asleep. It's dark and cold, and the men working ice wear hats and gloves and woolen leggings even on the hottest summer day. They're busy moving ice into the holds of ships lined up at the wharf, but not too busy to set a frozen chunk of winter into the back of our wagon.

Mama measures cream and sugar into the can of the ice cream freezer while I carefully pour in the cocoa. Papa chips the ice and packs it around the can with layers of salt. Then I start to turn the crank. It turns easily at first, gentle strokes swirling chocolate, cream, and sugar round and round the dasher. But as the cream begins to freeze my arm grows tired and the crank turns slow and slower until I can't turn it at all. Then Mama takes over and cranks until the ice cream is so hard the dasher won't turn another inch. When that happens, Mama sets the can on ice to keep until dinner and gives me the dasher to lick.

As I sit on the kitchen step licking chocolate from the ice-cold dasher, I close my eyes and imagine the island of always-summer, where giant pink seashells line the beaches and children pick chocolate from trees.

THE COCOA ICE TRADE

Chocolate really does grow on trees in the rain forests of Central America. Ancient Mayan Indians were the first to pick the cacao pods and turn them into a hot drink just the way the Dominican family does in *Cocoa Ice*. Except that ancient Mayan Indians didn't use sugar in their hot chocolate. Before Columbus crossed the Atlantic, only people in the Old World knew about sugar, and only people in the New World knew about chocolate.

Even after the Native Americans gave hot cocoa and cocoa beans to Europeans, farmers around London and Boston could not grow cacao trees. Chocolate grows only in tropical places, just as water turns into ice only in cold places like Maine. In the 1870s, Yankee trading schooners brought ice, manufactured goods, and refined sugar to Santo Domingo to trade for cocoa and coffee beans. Which meant that children in Santo Domingo and children in Maine could eat chocolate ices on lazy summer afternoons, just as they do in this story.

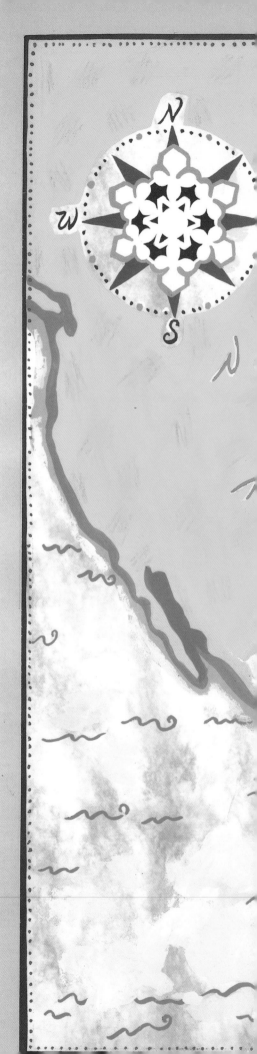

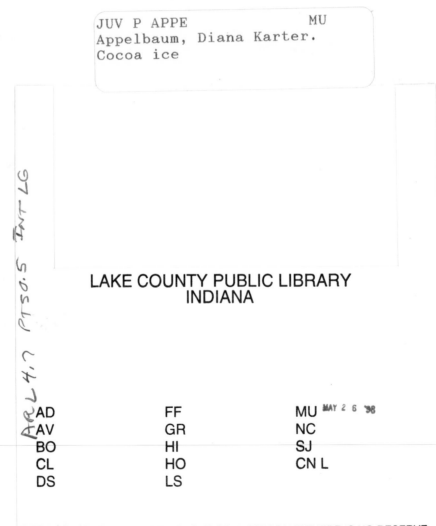